Tina Hughes was born and raised in Gloucestershire. The author re-located in 1986 with her husband and son to Bahrain, where she spent many years working as a teacher assistant in a primary school and then later established an art studio where she taught adults various techniques, chiefly involving stained glass and mosaics. During a marriage breakdown, Tina moved back to the UK, where she now lives with her new husband on their 11-acre plot on a remote hillside in Wales.

Dedicated to my friend, Anne, whose memory becomes more treasured with every passing year.

Tina Hughes

TALES OF TYNANT

AUSTIN MACAULEY PUBLISHERS™

LONDON · CAMBRIDGE · NEW YORK · SHARJAH

A CIP catalogue record for this title is available from the British Library.

ISBN 9781528960533 (Paperback)
ISBN 9781528961639 (ePub e-book)

www.austinmacauley.com

First Published 2023
Austin Macauley Publishers Ltd®
1 Canada Square
Canary Wharf
London
E14 5AA

With thanks to my husband, Rob, for his endless patience and support.

Table of Contents

Introduction

In the 1980s, Rob and his wife, Anne, went on a hunt to buy a suitable project property with enough land on which to live 'the good life' during their retirement in the distant future. After months of searching and ever-widening their circle away from their ancestral homes in Shropshire, they found Tynant in mid-Wales. It was an abandoned farm, on a windswept hillside, with views of the Cambrian Mountains. The house, a derelict, tumble-down wreck, had a tree growing in the middle where the roof had been and was reaching skyward to peer out at the world. Obscured by willows and having a rocky, winding track of a drive and a long-forgotten barn, it was the perfect place.

Living and working abroad made nothing easy when it came to acquiring planning permission, and a few times, Rob had to make special journeys to attend site meetings only to have it refused, twice. As with many things, though, persistence paid off, and they finally got it. However, it came with conditions, of course. Two original walls had to remain. The windows had to be in keeping with the originals—small, wooden and painted. The roof had to be tiled in Welsh slate, and the entire building could not be enlarged much more than the original footprint.

Making enquiries at a local tractor servicing centre, a local builder named Gilbert was recommended. He turned out to be an honest, forthright and hard-working man. As well as a builder, he became a project manager and in many ways, an architect too, putting his own mark on this beautiful home and has since become a trusted friend and confidant.

From the day Rob and Anne purchased the property until the day it was ready to move into, 25 years had passed. Visiting a couple of times a year, progress was slow but sure, and gradually, they began changing the surrounding land. The dirt track became a recognised drive. Part of the forest of willows next to the house had been removed and in a soggy dip. A pond was dug out and within a week it was full of water, runoff from the surrounding fields and looked like it had always been there.

In between their visits, Rob and Anne lived and worked in the Middle East. I did too, and it was during my employment at a school there that I met Anne and their daughter, Rachel, who was a teacher there. Over the years, our families became friends. Year after year, summer holidays ended and new school terms began, and Anne would tell me of the progress made at Tynant and showed me photos of the pond and when the roof was put on and told of the planting of a couple of hundred trees along the drive and gave me an open invitation to visit anytime they were there. This was how it went until the summer of 2016.

Anne's health hadn't been so good for a number of years, and she had a procedure scheduled to take place. Whilst in hospital, she contracted pneumonia and with other complications, she, very sadly, didn't make it. In the meantime, I was on my annual leave and visiting family in

Gloucestershire. I and my husband of 40 years had been going through a rough patch, but he assured me that all would be well, and once I'd returned from my visit, we would put it all behind us. This did not turn out to be the case, and after a few weeks, he arrived at the conclusion that the best thing for him, at least, was to go cold turkey and cut me out of his life. I was devastated and for a long time in denial and told lies and made excuses to friends and family about why I had not returned after the holidays. Both my life and Rob's had been turned upside-down. We were two very lonely, very traumatised people. Rob and Anne's families had gathered together for support and also for her lovely send-off which I attended.

One month later, I texted Rachel and asked how the family was coping. She told me that they had all returned to their homes and jobs and were doing the best they could, all except for Rob, who remained at the family home in Shropshire. She was concerned about him struggling to cope alone and, at my request, she gave me his number. I called him straight away, and we chatted awhile and arranged to meet for lunch that day. I didn't let on that my own situation had changed and anyway, at that stage, I was still clinging to the hope that all would be well. Over the next few months, we met quite often, and eventually, I told Rob how my marriage had ended. With the passing of time, we had grown close and one day came to the realization that we had, in fact, accidentally fallen in love and could no longer do the 'goodbyes'. We wrestled with the notion that people might talk, and indeed some did, but then, what were the rules? Who says we should be alone and lonely and for how long? In the end, we just did what felt right for us, and our families were so supportive and happy that we had found comfort in each other.

One day, Rob asked me to come to Wales with him and see Tynant before he sold it. It was a great pity, as so much had been invested in it. It had been caringly and lovingly built out of next to nothing, and the sad thing was that it hadn't even been properly lived in, all except for a few snatched days and nights here and there. Rob had already spoken with an estate agent, and it was about to go on the market. I'd never travelled that far into Wales before and was completely awestruck by the spectacular scenery. We arrived after a couple of hours of twisty, winding roads around rugged mountains and miles of conifer forests.

"So, this is it then," I said. "I remember seeing photos from years ago. It's so beautiful."

"Well, I can't live here alone," said Rob. "Could you live here with me?"

The Pond

The pond covers an area of around a quarter of an acre and was dug out due to the perpetually soggy earth in that particular spot. It is lined with clay and fills from the run off of the surrounding hills and an overflow pipe takes the excess water to one of two natural streams that run through the garden. It is currently two thirds covered by a weed which we would like to get rid of, so we need to find the safest way to do that. Last year we raked a lot of it out but we think that by breaking the plant beneath the surface, we've just encouraged it to bush out and thrive. There are several reed types that grow around the edges and many wild flowers, most notably irises, water mint, forget-me-nots and water marigolds to name but a few.

A bucketful of white water-lilies were emptied into the pond many years ago by Rob's dad which are thriving and always put on a good show from June onwards. The kidney-shaped island in the middle is overgrown with foxgloves, ferns and arrowhead reeds. There never seems to be a good time to go there and sort it out. From early spring, it becomes a nesting site for moorhens, mallards and Canada geese and a stopover for grey lag geese and even swans.

Two years ago, in the depths of winter, the entire surface of the pond became frozen and had been so for several days, and the ice was a good couple of inches thick. One white and frosty morning, at first light, I looked out of the window and saw a hungry fox had ventured across the ice and had found breakfast on the island. I watched him through my binoculars, tugging and tearing at something before having a quick chew and swallowing it down. He carried some more food across the snow-covered ice to eat on the raised bank near the edge, leaving a line of footprints as he went then again, back to the island to retrieve the remainder. Quite what it was, I couldn't see. I wondered if the ice would hold his weight, but I think the beautiful copper-brown of his coat belied the fact that he was very young and probably only weighed a few kilos. Looking around, with his bright amber eyes as if to check that no one might come and steal his food, he gulped down the last few bites and, seemingly satisfied, trotted off over the brow of the hill, nose sniffing the clean crisp air as he went. I watched him until the black tip of his bushy tail had disappeared out of sight.

As winter fades and makes way for spring, the ice melts and the water becomes warmer. The pond is full of activity again as the little aquatic creatures come out of hibernation. If you are quiet as you walk around on a warm, sunny afternoon, you can see all the little frogs gathering in the shallows. Scores of them, all clambering over one another, in a writhing, croaking mass of a mating frenzy. Any sudden moves and the whole lot of them will dive for cover beneath the surface and you will have to wait patiently without moving a muscle for a good fifteen minutes before they resume. A day or two later, bucketfuls of spawn are seen in and around the edges of the pond and a couple of weeks after that, tadpoles, huge metre-wide swathes of them, slowly, stretching across from one bank to the other, all sparkling in the sunlight and splashing in the water as if competing for space, although in reality, there is plenty.

It's around this time that the herons become more frequent visitors. They mostly arrive alone, but sometimes they come in pairs. They look so elegant, patiently standing there, statuesque in attitude, in what appears to be their best morning suits with their long, pointed beaks, poised at the ready for an unsuspecting snack to wander by.

In the early spring, when the wild fowl arrive for nesting, so do the mink and the otters. The mink, a rather beautiful-looking, long and slinky creature, is a terrible pest. Imported many decades ago, it's no longer a popular practice, not in Britain anyway, to wear fur coats. The creatures either escaped or were released from the farms and now run rampant in the UK's waterways, murdering water-voles (They don't eat them.) and biting the brains out of fish.

Every year, we have visiting otters. They are protected by law and, as such, breed freely in our waterways. Many anglers have noted these habitually nocturnal animals appearing by day to hunt their prey. They will eat fish, frogs, eggs and birds and come over the land to feast on the fruits of the pond. Adults can be the size of dogs, and I have seen them move torpedo-like through the water and strike a fully grown Canada goose and drag it down beneath the surface without struggle or sound, to be devoured at leisure I know not where. Almost a whole family of two adults and four adolescent goslings were preyed upon in this way last summer. It's the natural way of things, we know, but we found it upsetting and so discouraged the geese that arrived this year, selfishly sparing ourselves the trauma. We helped one gosling escape by persistently chasing it into the sheep field over the fence. It seemed to be making friends with the sheep and I witnessed it grazing alongside them for at least a fortnight. Then one day, the sheep were rounded up and taken away for dipping, and the gosling flew away.

In midsummer, we have umpteen neon-blue damsel flies and several golden ringed dragonflies skimming over the water. The dragonflies have big, bright green eyes and black and golden-yellow rings the length of their bodies. The males are 74 mm and the females 84 mm long. On warm days, they can be seen hovering up to a metre or more above the pond surface. They often chase one another, stopping frequently and briefly on the reeds and lily pads. There are a myriad of other flies and beetles in and on the pond, of which I know little, except to say they are all prone to be someone's next meal sooner or later.

As we move into autumn, the once-diminished water levels begin to rise again as the days become cooler and wetter. The once-lush green of the reeds and grasses start to fade. The water lilies begin to decay and the pondweed slowly browns and disappears. The swallows, now well practiced in dipping and diving, have departed on their long-haul back to Africa and flocks of starlings replace them with their overhead murmurings before landing *en masse* on the hillside. The foxes reappear, sniffing about the reeds. They will soon be calling across the pond at night, looking for a mate. One by one, the creatures find their watery beds in which to see out the winter, and day by day, the once-lively arena seems to silently go to sleep.

The Woodshed

The woodshed was built in a week by Gilbert Davies, the same man that built the house. It has a concrete floor and has gaps all around between the walls and roof to allow for airflow without letting in the rain, which means there is a generous overhang at one end and a wide doorway at the other.

Every year, as soon as we have a break in the weather and it's neither too wet nor icy, Rob goes out and finds trees to cut down, and the property has plenty of overgrown, fallen down willows, so they're not difficult to find. He cuts the trees into logs about 15 inches long, which fit nicely onto the log splitter that I operate within the shed. Once split, I carefully stack the logs into the three bays, seven and a half feet deep and six feet high. We usually start the process of gathering our fuel in March and are finished by the end of April. This year was different, though. Firstly, the winter was a little colder and longer and was followed by two months of rain. It didn't really stop until May, and then it was all go getting the wood in to give it enough time to dry out before we could use it. We were hard at it, continuously for around three weeks. I find it tough going sometimes, as some of the logs are bigger and heavier to lift than others, but I always manage. I'm prone to carpel tunnel syndrome. It's most unpleasant and keeps me awake at night after a heavy working day. It soon passes, though, and after a week of stopping, it's as though nothing happened.

The woodshed is also home to the mower and my various gardening tools. Hanging up in the rafters is a reindeer I made out of chicken wire and string. It looks a little forlorn now and needs a revamp or the bin but it makes me smile, as it reminds me of Ahmed, the camel, I made at a school I once worked in, in the Middle East.

Often, when I'm working inside the shed, I've been watched over by a robin, its shiny, black eyes no doubt looking for grubs, spilling out as they often do, from the centre of a hollowed log. I occasionally uncover little vermicelli droppings amongst the wood, a tell-tale sign that mice sometimes take refuge from the weather. This, no doubt, prompts the visits from the barn owl whose runny, white excretions I find have been splashed with gusto across the cleanly swept floor like some sort of Pollock apprentice whose heart wasn't quite in it. One winter evening, Rob and I walked together up to the shed to collect more fuel for our fire. As we approached, we startled the owl. It glided out silently above our heads and disappeared into the dark night. What a treat to see him up close even for the briefest moment! He hasn't left any signs of visiting the shed recently, but we know he's around, as we've found the pellets he coughs up and we hear him when we're tucked up in our bed at night, with the window open. Imagine if he landed on the windowsill. Wouldn't that be something?

A Salopian Tale

When Rob still owned the house in Ludlow, we would often spend days there, catching up with family or doing jobs around the house in preparation for selling. We also occasionally went shopping. It was on a dull Tuesday morning that we set off for Shrewsbury to buy a suitable mirror to hang in the hallway of our home here in Wales, and in due course, we arrived at the shop where, sometime previously, we had seen a few that we liked. We chose a large, rectangular, wooden-framed mirror and, due to its size, needed assistance from a staff member to carry it out of the store and into the car and, feeling very pleased with our purchase, we drove back to Ludlow with it before going on to Wales. Once home, we unwrapped our mirror and our hearts sank as we realised there had been some mistake and this was not the one we chose at all. Oh, the disappointment! Well, no matter, we would take the mirror back next week when we planned on returning to Ludlow, as it isn't as far to Shrewsbury from there, as it is from home and since we were going anyway, well, you get the picture.

There we were then, a week later, at the house in Ludlow. We took the mirror with us and placed it near the front door at the bottom of the stairs. It was rather cumbersome, and although it was somewhat in the way, it saved us having to carry it further into the house. A few days passed and we decided to take it back to the store. I must explain here that, whereas Shrewsbury is only thirty miles away from Ludlow, it takes the best part of an hour to get there, as the A49 is a very busy and wiggly road. We had almost arrived at the store, and I mean 100 metres away, when I turned to look at the mirror, the great big mirror, in its box on the backseat.

"Um, Rob!" I said. "Where is the mirror?"

"What? What do you mean? Where is the mirror?" his voice raised with a slight hint of annoyance there already.

We both looked at each other in disbelief. We had travelled all this way on this tediously slow and busy road and we had forgotten to bring the bloody mirror! You can imagine the pain, the boredom and the shear absurdity of the situation. We didn't know whether to laugh or cry. We decided to laugh and drove straight back, got the mirror and again travelled the A49 to Shrewsbury and eventually bought a very different but beautiful one that we love and is hanging on our wall in Wales. Needless to say, we check everything now before we leave the store.

Roland's Walk

When we first came to live in our house in Wales, the garden was all a bit overgrown. A basic plan was there, but with all the travelling to and from the Middle East, Rob hadn't got round to taming it as such, so, when we moved here and made it our permanent residence, the first thing we did was to clear a path all the way around the pond, which is roughly a quarter of an acre in size with a kidney-shaped island in the centre. This was quite a task, as there were crack willows all over the place intertwined with hawthorn and brambles and all of it covered in knotted, long lengths of ivy. Most of the willows were on the house side of the pond. They were around two storeys tall and leant this way and that way and made a lovely, leafy canopy, and once we'd cleared the tangled mess beneath it, we were left with a straight path tunnelling east west-ish for about 60 metres through the trees. It had quite a pull for me, standing at the western end of the path looking through to the east. I had to walk the length to see the magnificent view at the end as it opened out onto the brow of the hill and directly in sight of Cors Caron (an ancient bog) and the Cambrian Mountains beyond.

We've noticed that when you change something in the garden, so too are other, sometimes unintentional, changes made and with the advent of this pathway opening, a male pheasant suddenly appeared one day in winter. We first saw him through the gaps in the trees and the thought struck me that he could have been a small man, aged 40-something, ambling along, the epitome of sartorial elegance, having spent the night before at a country ball and was now, hands clasped behind his back, playfully contemplating how he might woo his newly found love along this very path. We named him Roland, and since he strolled along the said path every day, we called it Roland's walk.

In the spring, he made a habit of sitting on the low wall around the patio and, it seemed to us, patiently waited for us to enter the conservatory where we eat our breakfast. He would come right up to the door and look as much as to say, "Is breakfast being served yet?" Rob would open the door and Roland, overcome by nervousness, would run a few metres away. Then once Rob was back indoors, out he would come to enjoy his own especially served morsels before retiring to his big log at the side of the walk, which for all intents and purposes was his very own throne. Every so often, we saw him stand very tall, chest puffed out, head raised up, his beak opened and would shout, "Cuk-kuk!" at the top of his voice.

Roland has been coming and going over the years. We don't know if it's the same pheasant, but he gets called Roland anyway. We last saw him in late spring after an absence of a couple of weeks. He arrived early one morning and had his lady love with him. They looked very fine as they strutted up to the patio, Roland proudly treating her to the Tynant dining experience he's by now used to. They've since been away, no doubt honeymooning. I'm sure he'll be back in the autumn.

Whether or not Mrs Pheasant returns with him remains to be seen.

The Old Barn

The old barn, at a guess, is around 150 years old. Half of it is built of red brick, the other Welsh stone, and used to be a milking parlour for around a half dozen cows at a time. From this viewpoint, the vista is really rather breath-taking, as it encompasses most of the garden with the pond in the foreground and the Cambrian Mountains in the distance, but because of visible lack of fencing or roads, it's difficult to perceive where the garden ends in the miles of open countryside laid out before you. One could quite imagine being able to set out unhindered and hike to the highest point on the horizon.

Many years ago, Rob and Anne used the older stone section of the barn for storing all the wood needed to keep the fires lit over winter. That was until a couple of youngsters came by one day when no one was home and set it all alight. An estimated ten thousand pounds worth of damage was caused that day, not to mention all the man hours to cut, split and stack all the logs. The fire brigade came as soon as they could, but their best efforts couldn't save the old Welsh slate roof, but thankfully, nobody was hurt. The police caught the offenders but due to their young age, all that could be done was to tell them off. For years since then, the space has mainly been used for storing nothing more than the recycling.

Rob has always had the idea that one day, the barn would become two holiday cottages and a couple of years ago applied for planning permission. This was a lengthy process and was twice refused. On the third attempt however, we teamed up with a local young architect with fresh designs, but before submitting the plans to the planning department, we were told that it is the law of the land that any plans must be accompanied by an ecological survey report. To me and you, it means, see if you have any bats living in the barn, and in order to find that out, we had to employ the services of Batman. Well, not quite, but a bat man. He arrived one evening just before sunset and, armed with a clever little app on his smart device, he sat there detecting bat sounds. It turned out that we had two types flitting about our twilight garden but none were entering or exiting the barn. Batman said that at a glance, he knew without question that we wouldn't have bats in the barn because the tin roof would cook them on a sunny day, but he had to come back again, a three-hour drive, in a week's time to double-check, as is the requirement. In a conversation, I told him that a bat flew in through a bedroom window one evening, and although its presence interrupted our bedtime reading, we were delighted to see one up close and caught it with the aid of a thin cloth and put it back through the window. On hearing this, he took such a sharp intake of breath and told me that what I did was breaking the law. These bats are protected and I shouldn't have touched it but instead call the services of a qualified bat-handler. Not too long afterwards, our friends Pauline and Shanee came for a visit. They love the fresh air and like to have their room windows continuously open. Well, it didn't take long before very late one evening, as we were retiring to bed, Shanee called out with a shriek of absolute delight.

"There's a bat in my room!"

As she opened her bedroom door, the bat danced and zigzagged through the air from bedroom to landing to bathroom. Our joyful guests thought the whole spectacle was wonderful, but after a few minutes, we all thought it best to get the creature back outside where it belonged. It was then that I remembered the words of warning from the batman. I looked at my watch. It was one o'clock. The nearest bat-handler was a three-hour drive away. As I spent a second to consider what was best for the bat, our little friend landed on Shanee's shoulder. She was thrilled. I told her to keep still and, very slowly and carefully, I cupped my hands over it and ever so gently lifted it off and carried it to the window where, none the worse for being handled by one so terribly unqualified, it flew off into the dark night.

With the survey completed, we submitted our application to the planning department, and this time it was successful. The first thing we had to do was knock down the unsafe walls and dig out a trench that would become the footings for the new building. We decided to buy a digger for the purpose and searched for a second-hand one online. Rob found just the machine, and what a bargain price it was too! He phoned the seller and made arrangements for delivery and paid up-front. Then we waited and waited, but it never arrived, and after a little investigation, we experienced a horrible sinking feeling as we discovered that we had been scammed out of four thousand pounds by an online thief. It had all been done so cleverly and convincingly. We still needed a digger and this time proceeded with great caution. We found a seller operating on the same business park as my brother-in-law, Tony, so we asked Tony to check for us, and as it turned out, all was well and they even knew each other. The digger arrived and Rob soon set about knocking down the walls. My brother and his wife even came over and joined in the fun. Then came the hard work of digging out the footings. The digger alone couldn't do it. The ground was so hard and the rocks and boulders were too many. Rob had to buy an electric jackhammer and get in the trenches and do most of the work that way and then use the digger to scoop the loosened earth afterwards. As this stage of the work started, so did the rain. We all know that in UK, we probably get more than our fair share of it, but it becomes even more apparent when you have an outdoor activity that you really would like to be getting on with. This was the way of the weather for over a month, and it seemed that this relatively small job was never going to get finished, but of course it did. The trenches were filled with concrete and builders were contacted, and one day, where the old barn once stood, I'm sure we will have a beautiful little cottage.

The Swallows

The swallows arrive every year in mid-April. They use the old nests they made previously in the barn, high up in the rafters. There are usually two pairs. They lay around ten to a dozen eggs each. The young appear around the beginning of June and, shortly afterwards, make their exits all at once, circling round and round the house and gardens and then just as suddenly disappearing back into the barn. This is repeated several times a day. After a few days, they all take up positions on the overhead telephone wire and wait there for the parents to come hovering in front of them before pushing their catch of insects, caught on the wing, into their hungry, gaping mouths. Other times, they just sit—the whole family—in unison on their favourite wire, chattering away as if discussing the day's agenda before flying off for their pond-dipping lessons. It doesn't take long before they are all quite expert at hovering, dipping and eating on the wing.

They really are the most agile little birds and fast too. One day, whilst sitting in the conservatory, I saw a sparrow-hawk appear as if from nowhere and dive into the bird feeding area amongst the hazels in our garden. Whether it grabbed a small

bird or not, I couldn't tell, as it all happened so fast, but within seconds, a squadron of swallows were scrambled. They were very daring as they caught up with him, swooped down and pecked at him and chased him away down the hillside far beyond the garden.

Another day, as if for sport, I saw them dive-bomb a squirrel who was about to start foraging in one of the flower tubs on the patio. It looked most surprised at the rude interruption and ran for cover beneath an ornamental standard. Just yesterday, a magpie was standing on a wall and about to eat some crumbs when three vigilante swallows descended on him and gave his head a good pecking as they flew by, the magpie making hastc to the nearby ash tree for cover.

In the early autumn, the families of swallows gather together on the overhead wires in large numbers. They come from the surrounding areas, and when all are present, they set off on their incredibly long journey back home to Africa.

The Washing Line

Now, when I was a kid, my mum always had a washing line, a length of plastic-covered wire running along and above the path from the wall of the house to a post at the end of the garden. That's what I grew up with and that's what, as an adult, I've always had at my various homes, so, when I came to live in Wales and discovered that I was expected to use a 'whirly' version, my heart sank and I was instantly irritated by this awful contraption. I can understand that if one has a small garden and space is precious, then yes, maybe a whirly is a practical and reasonable answer to one's clothes-drying requirements, but we have oodles of space. Week after week, I complained about the ugly gadget.

"It spoils the view," I said.

"Well then, remove it when you're not using it," Rob suggested.

It wouldn't keep still when I tried pegging clothes onto it and some of the lines went slack after having heavy wet towels on it. The clothes wouldn't dry quickly and evenly because of the lack of space and airflow between the lines, and there simply wasn't a length long enough to hang sheets. We couldn't have it on the patio, as it would mean making a hole in one of the lovely tiles, so I'd get wet feet going to use it after it had rained. After I'd used it, I would stow it away out of sight behind the house, and when I wanted to use it again, I couldn't find the hole it stood in because the grass had grown over it. I placed an upturned flowerpot over the hole, which I then had to remember to remove before I mowed the grass. Otherwise when I got off mid-mow, the mower would stop and wasn't always so easy to restart. Then, there were the spiders. If it spent any longer than a couple of days round the back of the house, the spiders would move in and come abseiling out the minute I opened the arms of the thing. I complained about the dreadful thing for almost four years. I was quite capable of installing a proper line myself, but we have this thing where we must both agree to everything, well, most things anyway, and besides, I don't think Rob entirely trusts me to mix concrete properly. Anyway, at long last, I was heard. I DON'T LIKE WHIRLY WASHING LINES!

One day, postie delivered two washing posts, one with a pulley and cleat and one plain and a nice, long, single-length of line. Rob put it up in a jiffy. No fuss or bother or big preparations. *Boom!* There it was, running along and above the path in the garden at the side of the house. I found a long hazel branch with a fork at one end to serve as a prop and have been as happy as Larry ever since. I find something mildly satisfying and therapeutic about pegging out my washing as I was taught back in the day by my mother and grandmother. It's part of the way things were, and I do like to hang onto a little bit of that.

The Wedding and the Weather

Having just got engaged, the next thing Rob and I had to concentrate on was when to have our wedding. The question of 'where' didn't occur, as it was obvious. Our home was sufficient to accommodate the closest family and the garden with its beautiful Cambrian Mountain views would be perfect for the all-important photos. We thought long and hard about the timing. Winter? Too cold. Spring and Autumn? Too rainy. Late Summer? Too rainy. The previous couple of Junes had been good, and so we went with that.

We soon discovered that when planning a wedding, the mere mention of it hikes up the prices. Now whereas we don't mind paying a decent price for decent service, we did feel in the main that we were about to get right royally, ripped off, so it didn't take us long to decide that we were going to go D.I.Y. We began gathering wedding essentials like a marquee, music speaker and ice buckets and arranged tables and chairs and all sorts of other paraphernalia one needs to make the day a great success.

We had most things organized, and five days prior to tying the knot, Rob and I decided that as it was such a fine, windless day. It was time to put up the marquee. We are a good team and were doing quite well but hadn't anticipated the weight when lifting the roof section in order to attach the legs. Not wanting to give up, we tried lifting part legs onto chairs first, hoping then to attach the bottom parts, but we simply weren't strong enough. We were just about to admit defeat when along came Rob's son, Ryan. He, Nadia and Kaya had arrived a couple of weeks earlier and had been out visiting friends. That extra pair of hands were all that was needed. However, as we came to the final stages of erection, the heavens opened with such ferocity that none of us could ever recall a storm in Wales quite like it. At one point, a now-slate-coloured cloud directly overhead billowed so low; it was getting hard to distinguish between it and the roof, and from somewhere within its fully charged interior came a blinding flash and a crash of thunder. We shrieked and screamed as we all dashed for the cover of the house and waited breathlessly for it to pass. The rain poured across the patio and inside the marquee. We had visions of guests with wet feet and dripping hems, and the next day, Rob did his best to stave it all off with expanding foam sprayed along the edges of the ground bars. The rain continued for the next few days, and I was fast losing any hope of outdoor photos in our beautiful garden with the wonderful views.

One by one, Rob's family arrived for our wedding in Aberystwyth. The clouds parted and the sun came out. What a beautiful day we had! That evening, my sister and her fiancé arrived and then my other sister with her husband followed by my brother and his wife the next day. Then all the other family and friends came for the big celebration in the marquee in the garden. In stark contrast to earlier in the week, the weather had become quite hot and some guests even got sunburnt! I was cool in my cream cotton dress and, with my wonderful prince beside me, didn't have a care in the world. The photos were lovely and scenic. The food was delicious, and the drinks were aplenty as we danced, laughed and loved our company. It all turned out perfect.

The Slug

We all know that siblings all over the world are, at any age, inclined to prank one another, and we're no different in our family. One weekend, my younger sisters, Polly and Dawne, came for a visit. We all had a lovely time shopping, chatting over lunch and generally catching up, and after a fabulous few days together, we hugged, kissed and said our goodbyes and they set off on the three-hour drive back to their own homes and families. After having waved them out of sight, as is customary, I returned indoors and went up the stairs where, on the banister rail, I saw a very large slug. My first reaction was an instinctive revolt. I don't mind seeing them outside, but in my house, eeugh! I stared at it for a second in disbelief and quickly concluded it was not real and had been placed there by one of my sisters. I wondered which one.

A few hours went by and I called Dawne to check that she and Polly had arrived home okay and without incident. She said that they had and thanked me once again for a lovely weekend. I then told her that after they had left, I'd found the most enormous slug in the house.

"It is gigantic!" I exclaimed.

"Oh goodness!" said she, sounding only mildly interested. "What did you do?"

"I picked it up with a tissue and threw it out of the window."

"Oh," she mumbled. She honestly couldn't have sounded more bored with the conversation if she'd been paid to try.

Ah ha! I thought, *So, Polly did it.*

I decided not to speak of it anymore, and since she had hoped to scare *me* with it, I would get my revenge all in good time. So, I put the thing in a drawer and forgot all about it.

Several weeks passed by and then Polly got in touch to say that she and Tony, the new man in her life, would like to come over for the weekend. I soon thought about the slug and rubbed my hands together and giggled at the thought of passing back the prank, except that I would do a better job of it. I had the idea of putting it in their bed, but I didn't know Tony well enough, and for all I knew, he could have some previous trauma caused by slugs or a phobia even and might have a seizure or something. (I watch *YouTube*. I know about these things.) No, whatever I did, I had to prank responsibly. I waited until we were all together, and Polly and Tony were deep in conversation with Rob when I slipped away upstairs

to retrieve the slug from the drawer. I tiptoed into the guest bedroom and wondered on which side of the divan Polly had been sleeping. Then, I spied her handbag on the wooden floor next to the bed and carefully placed the slug beside it and went back downstairs, feeling rather pleased with myself. We were all having a lovely chat when eventually Polly needed to go upstairs to fetch something from her bag. I surreptitiously followed and waited with the side of my hand on my mouth, stifling my laughter, and listened for the inevitable scream.

I could hold back no longer and laughed out loud and ran up the stairs. Polly was by now laughing too and asked if it was me that had planted the slug there. I told her I had and inquired as to whether she recognised it. I saw the puzzled look on her face and then the penny dropped as she remembered.

"Yes," she said. "I was with Dawne when she bought it. It was when I was last here. She thought it would be fun to play a prank on you."

Poor old Polly! I didn't feel too bad though, as I know she probably wished she had thought of it and she did see the funny side of it.

I kept the slug on one of the windowsills for a while until Rob's son Ryan, his wife, Nadia, and their then three-year-old daughter Kaya came to stay for their summer holidays. Kaya loves the outdoors and will spend hours watching dragonflies, frogs, spiders and beetles. She's fascinated by all of the creatures. One morning, I handed her the realistic-looking slug. She loved it and because of its comparative size to others she had seen in the garden, she named it 'Grandpa Slug'. She played with it every day, bathing it in the birdbath and even took it with her at bedtime. She became quite attached to it and so, when the holiday was over and it was time to go home, of course, the slug went too.

The Cable Guy

The internet connection here, at best, is pretty bad, so when it got down to non-existent, we knew we had better do something about it. Once our complaint was heard, a couple of days later, a man turned up. It was on the morning of one of the wettest days we'd ever seen, and yet, there he was all smiles as if he'd just been invited out to afternoon tea at the Ritz. He tested this and tested that and then announced that the problem was that one of the willows had been rubbing on the cable, causing it to wear thin and we needed to trim the tree back in order to delay any further immediate damage. A prognosticator that Rob is, he could see immediately that the complete removal of the tree was called for and before the man had chance to dream up any delay, as if by magic, it had whipped out his chainsaw.

"Trouble is it's going to crash onto the cable and snap it," said Rob.

"No it won't. You'd be surprised how strong these cables are," said the man.

In spite of the howling winds and torrential rain, Rob set to with his chainsaw. The tree swayed and creaked and all at once crashed down onto the cable and snapped it with a very audible whippish-sounding crack. Well, that did it! Since the man was already here and had miles of cable with him, he got onto installing a new one right away.

I watched the man high up on the pole and felt sorry for him having to come out in weather like this to fix a cable. It wasn't as if our lives depended on it. It could have waited another day, but I mused at how very happy he looked up there.

The rain was coming down so hard and fast now that looking on from the comfort of my conservatory window, he was, but for his bright orange jacket, barely visible. Yet, he seemed to take his time and had the composure of someone serving up ice creams on a Caribbean beach. Rob, on the other hand, was very miffed, but not being one for giving up, he was determined to get the tree all sawn up into logs and stacked in an orderly fashion before returning to the comfort of the house.

The wind was now howling like a banshee and the rain came down harder than ever. Rob's ears were taking a lashing and cold rivulets made their way down the back of his neck and soaked his shirt. After the twenty minutes or so it took to finish sawing, my poor old husband looked for all the world like someone who had had one ride to many on the log flume at a theme park. The man, having the task finished, was packing up his tools and loading them into the back of his van. I offered him a hot drink.

"I've brought my own, thanks," he said, showing me his thermos flask as he climbed in behind his steering wheel.

"I don't think I've ever seen a more cheerful-looking man going about his work and in such awful weather," I said, smiling back at him.

He gave a little chuckle and told me he was new on the job.

"I've just left the army and was in Afghanistan the other week," he said and, still smiling, drove away.

Those Magnificent Men

When I was little and my esteemed grandfather was in the Royal Air Force, he and my grandmother, along with two of my uncles and three of my aunts, were posted to Bahrain. My mum missed them greatly and whenever we were outside playing in the garden and a plane passed overhead, it would remind her that they had left the country and flown far away and she would encourage me and my younger brother to wave at the plane and say, "Goodbye, Nana and Grandad." Now whether it was doing that at such a young age (I must have been three or four years old at the time.) or the fact that my dad and most of my uncles had all served in the R.A.F and maybe it's got a little bit into my bones, I just don't know, but whenever I see an R.A.F plane fly by, I feel compelled to wave at it.

Living here, on our Welsh hillside, we've discovered that we seem to be on a flight-training path. Those pilots don't appear to like getting their planes wet, but on a sunny day, more often than not, those 'magnificent men in their flying machines' come and give us a good show, and they almost always come in pairs. Now, in order to be seen more clearly by the pilot of a jet fighter that is cruising passed at the speed of sound, I get out of my bright pink hoodie, run to the highest point in the garden and wave it frantically about whilst yelling, "Woooohooo!" at the top of my voice.

It was on one of those days when the sky is so vast and blue that I heard that sound you hear when a jet is approaching. The sort of sound you might get by sucking air through a large open straw but a million times louder. They fly so low that from one area in the garden, they're obscured by the hill, and so, you don't see them until they're above you. However, when coming in from the other side, the view is very open and they can be seen approaching from across the valley. It's then that I have enough time, if I'm very quick, to grab my hoodie and run.

On one particular occasion, the pilots had flown over us at least six times, flying low and high and twisting and turning, with me all the while waving my hoodie and yelling with excitement. What a wonderful show we had! On the last fly by, one of the pilots came swooping down, barely above the treetops, and flipped sideways so that I could clearly see him waving back at me. Then in the blink of an eye, he levelled up and disappeared out of sight and over the mountains.

Unexpected Visitors

Since living here at Tynant, we've been quite surprised at the number of people who have driven down our long drive without invitation and up to our house. It bothered me a little to begin with, well, you do hear stories, but since having the security systems installed, I no longer find it an issue. We've had several visits from well-meaning people, who turn up in twos and always open a conversation with a compliment about our garden or the view before getting down to the more serious subject of saving our souls. Then there are the sellers of fish from the back of a van and the same with meat. Apart from the obvious 'back of a van' red lights and sirens going off in my head, there's the issue of hygiene too. There was not an apron or hairnet in sight, never mind hand washing. No, thank you very much, you jog on, matey. Not touching that! Then there was the man selling logs and a highly suspicious-looking character who had eyes like weasels and asked if we would like to sell any machinery. I let this one see that I was noting down his vehicle registration number and asked for his name—just in case.

One day, a very interesting man appeared in the garden from the RSPB. We didn't hear him drive up, and he found me tidying up in the shrubbery. He wanted permission to explore the willows near to the stream. He was trying to track down willow warblers. They are small birds whose habitat, so I learnt, is under threat. It seems they were alive and well in our garden. I wasn't surprised as the willows grow like weeds around here. After making his report, the gentleman left and said he'd like to come back another time if that was quite okay.

We've had several visitors at different times looking for a particular barn, and I think perhaps it could be a wedding or some other social venue, and one day, we had a young man standing on our doorstep in the pouring rain, asking if this was where the party was! When we asked whose party and the address given, he didn't know!

On a particularly cold, wet and very windy November afternoon, we were startled to see an elderly man dressed in a long mac, looking for all the world like the '70s TV detective 'Colombo' peering in through our conservatory window and observing us enjoying an afternoon tea. We gestured to him with flapping arms and mouthed in a half-spoken half-breathed sort of way to, "Go back to the front door." When we opened the door to speak to him, we became quite discombobulated as he began to utter words in a very strange-sounding language that neither of our well-travelled ears had ever before heard. All we could think to do was make that 'I dunno' face and shrug. We now noticed that in his car sat an equally elderly lady, we assumed his wife, who looked just as hopeless as we did. We guessed they were looking for direction, and so we gestured some more and pointed to the road that goes up and over the hill. They both looked suddenly very satisfied with this and Colombo jumped into the driver's seat, and with big smiles, much nodding and jolly waves, off they went on their way to goodness knows where.

My favourite unexpected arrival came one warm summer's evening. Rob and I were sipping our way through a bottle of merlot and chatting about old times in our favourite spot outside under the pergola. As we gazed across the pond, watching the dab chicks foraging in the reeds, we heard the slow approach of a car and the gravel being crunched under the tyres. Into view appeared a beautiful, blush-pink sports car with the top down. We strolled along to meet the car as it came to a halt near the front door. The driver, a theatrical-looking partonesque woman in a tightfitting purple sequined maxi dress climbed out and, with one hand tidying her hair and a voice more camp than Butlins, said, "Am I at the right place? I'm not, am I? Are you Amanda and Shane? Is this Amanda and Shane's place?"

Not being able to get a word in, we just shook our heads.

"It's not is it?" he, as we now realised, continued and before we had chance to say anything, "Oh, em, gee! You wouldn't believe the day I'm having. Everything's been going wrong. I only got off the plane from Gran Canaria this morning. What a week that's been, I can tell you! I wasn't on holiday either. I've been working. Work, work, work, that's me though. I love it really. I'm working tonight as well. Well, meant to be, if I can find the blimin' place, but one look at your faces and I could tell I'm at the wrong address. I'm a drag act by the way. Well, you probably guessed. Look, this is the address I've been given." This poor man had only half a postcode in his sat nav, and we had never heard of the address, which was also incomplete.

"That half a code is surely South Wales somewhere," I said, trying to sound helpful.

His humungous long lashes fluttered as he blinked and revealed in full the pink, thick glitter eye shadow and then:

"Oh my God, oh my God, wait. Oh no, hang on a sec." He got back in his car, fumbled inside a large, brown, soft leather drawstring bag he had slung on the passenger seat and found a handwritten note on a tatty piece of paper. Carefully unfolding it, the address in its entirety was revealed. It was in a place called Velfrey, an hour-and-a-half drive away. He could still make it on time. He'd never heard of the place before, saying he wasn't from around here and, in his best Kidderminster accent, said that he 'Hails from Kidday'.

He thanked us both, for what, we're not sure, and said,

"This would be the perfect setting for a gig, if you ever decide to have a party here," and handed me his card.

"Dixie Devine—Drag Entertainer"

Surprise!

It was New Year's Day and our mutual friend Pauline had been visiting over the holidays. She, Rob and I were clearing away after breakfast, having spent the night before drinking, chatting and seeing the New Year in with Jules Holland on the tele when Rob's phone rang. I assumed it was one of our families calling to wish us a happy new year. He looked at the screen and quickly went into the next room, and when he returned to the kitchen, his face looked suddenly as if he had just been presented with some huge conundrum.

"Is everything okay?" I asked. Then Pauline joined in.

"What's wrong?"

"Um, well, I just have to pop out for a few hours."

"To where?" I quizzed.

"Umm, er, well, look, I'll tell you later." I felt a rising sense of nervousness come from within me.

"Later?" I asked, "What's going on? What's happened?"

"Nothing, darling. I just need to go out."

"But where to? Oh my God, are the kids all okay?"

"Yes, they're all fine, I promise. Everything is fine and I'll be back soon and will tell you all about it."

He gave me a reassuring hug.

"Okay," I said, "But I don't like it. You're scaring me. Is it that you don't want to tell me in front of Pauline?" I whispered.

"No, please, don't be afraid. Be happy. It's something nice."

"Are you going to town? To Aberystwyth?"

"Something like that," he said. By now, he had his shoes and coat on and, picking up the car keys, said he'd be back soon and got in the car and was away down our long drive.

I swung round to face Pauline.

"Where's he going?" I demanded.

"I don't know. I know nothing about it." I looked her square in the eyes. I'd know if she was lying.

"Are you sure?"

"I'm telling you," came her firm reply whilst also looking directly into my eyes, knowing very well what I was looking for. She was telling the truth. I ran up the stairs to the window where I could see the road running in both directions. I saw the car approach the gate. *Now would he turn left or right?* I thought.

"Pauline! Pauline, he's turned left," I called. "He's lying. He's not going to town at all. He's turned the other way."

"Really? Well, what's that way then?"

"Home, I mean our families' homes in England. Why is he going that way? Think Tina, think."

"Why don't you make us both a nice cup of tea? I think you need to calm down. You're getting yourself in a tiz."

"No, I'm not," I muttered, reaching for the kettle, knowing jolly well she was right.

"Oh, I'm going upstairs to start my packing. Call me when the tea's made." And with a chuckle, she disappeared upstairs.

I started thinking again more quickly now that I was alone. *Why that way? What's that way? Family, but he can't be going to visit family; it would take much longer than a couple of hours. Maybe someone is coming here! Maybe someone is coming here and he's going to meet them. Why go to meet them? They all know how to get here by now, except, except for Alex and Louise!*

My son and his wife had only been here once before when they came over from New Zealand where they used to live. They were back in the country now and yes, I thought, that must be it! Rob and I had discussed earlier in the year that when they came again, we would meet them an hour away from here to make sure that the Sat Nav didn't take them over any of those mountain roads that are beautiful in the summer but can be treacherous in the winter.

The tea was ready. I gave Pauline a call and she came to the kitchen and sat with me up at the table.

"Pauline, I've figured it out."

"Okay. Let's hear it."

"He's gone to meet Alex and Louise." And I explained my reasoning.

"But you don't know that!" she said, eyes wide in disbelief.

"Yes I do."

"What if you're wrong? You'll be so disappointed."

"I'm not wrong. I bet you."

"But he might be going to fetch something for you and then the disappointment will be written all over your face and you'll spoil the surprise for him." She was pouting now and feeling sorry for Rob.

"Nope," I insisted. "He's going to fetch Alex and Louise." Jumping up, I felt very pleased with myself and my amazing detective skills. *Move over Poirot,* I mused, *I'll take it from here.*

"I'm going to make sure the spare room is in order." I announced, heading for the stairs. "What shall I make us all for dinner?" I was really getting excited now and couldn't possibly sit still.

"I'm going to pack. I can't stand it," chuckled Pauline, taking her tea with her. She could see it was quite useless to try and make me see reason and it would all turn out however it was going to turn out, and there was nothing she could do.

The time was flying. I made some rough calculations in my head. It would take an hour to arrive at the rendezvous. Rob, being Rob, would arrive ten minutes early and Alex, being Alex, would arrive on time and then another hour to drive back again.

"They should be arriving about now!" I called out to Pauline and ran up the stairs and to the window to view the road. I wasn't there long when I saw our car appear from around the bend in the distance followed by another car that looked remarkably like Alex and Louise's.

"Ah ha! Hahaha!" I laughed aloud. "Come and see, Pauline; I was right!" I ran out onto the landing and did a little happy dance whilst Pauline was looking out in disbelief at the two cars turning into our drive. I ran downstairs, jumped into my wellies, being the fastest footwear to get on, and ran outside and laughed as I ran past Rob coming along the drive. Alex had hung back for more effect and to give Rob chance to spin some yarn and give the surprise more impact.

"Where are you going?" Rob shouted to me.

"To meet Alex and Louise," I laughed as I continued running.

Rob sat in silence, his jaw dropped, and then with a very puzzled look on his face, he asked,

"How the heck did you know that?"

"I'm Poirot. Don't you know? I can figure out anything." I laughed and went to grab my longed-for hugs from my son and his wife.

Cha-Cha

Anyone who knows me knows I am a lover of pussy cats. In the past, I've loved and kept ten of them, not all at once, though. For example, one time, there were four together and another time, just one. When I came to live with Rob, circumstances were such that I had to leave my precious pussies where they lived in Bahrain, and sadly, I've never seen them since. Cats being cats, I'm sure they don't miss me at all, and I know they were being well looked after by my ex-husband.

One evening, just as the setting sun had cast the last of its fading rose-gold rays across the now-dew-glistened grass, Rob, turning to me, with all the romantic charm of Quixote, asked,

"Would you like a horse, darling?"

Now, whereas I might be inclined to admire a beautiful horse or ride one or give one a friendly pat, actually owning one is another thing. I declined the offer but remarked that he was so kind and sweet and such a darling wanting only to please me. As time went by, after a year or so, when we both felt settled and more used to each other and our new lives together, I found I missed my pussy cats and asked Rob if he would agree to me getting one locally.

"Certainly not!" came his rather too swift and firm reply. "They drop hair and claw the furniture, and I'm not having it!"

"But you once asked me if I'd like a bloomin' horse," I wailed.

I tried pouting and feigning a sulk, all to no avail. I tried again when my birthday came around, but the answer was still no. I argued the benefits of keeping cats. No mice or squirrels, no voles tunnelling everywhere, but no; he wouldn't yield.

Christmas came and I'd long given up the idea of having another pussy cat. Under the tree were a couple of presents with my name on them and, one at a time, Rob handed them to me with that joyful expression he has on his face when he knows he's done something well or, in this case, knew I would love the gifts. The last gift was brought in from another room and was in a fancy-looking cardboard bag that had been tied at the top with a white satin ribbon. His face changed as he passed me this last one; it had mischief written all over it and he could barely contain his laughter. I looked at him quizzically. What could it be? As I peeked inside, amongst the tissue wrappings, I saw, quite plainly, black and white fur. For a second, my heart flew into my mouth. In the next second, I knew it was trickery. I opened the bag and there was a very beautiful, warm and cuddly, soft and furry toy cat. Oh, Rob was very pleased with himself and, throwing his head back, laughed a good, long, hearty laugh. He'd got me a black and white one too, like I had asked for. I saw the joke and, after giving him a playful slap, sat down with my lovely pussy that I named Cha-Cha and gave her a gentle stroke. I kept her in our bedroom for over a year and had great fun with it, tucking it in under our duvet after I had made the bed or put my glasses on her head and that sort of thing. When the grandchildren came to stay, I dressed her up with jewellery and scarves and sat her upright, with my glasses on her and put a book across her, as if reading. We did have a giggle when the then-three-year-old Lily looked at me and, with a big grin, said, "This is so silly, isn't it?"

Cha-Cha now lives in one of the guestrooms along with my other very much-loved soft toys—Chi-Chi, the panda and Darling, the dog.

When my mother was here recently, she intimated that she might like to sleep in that guestroom and pointed to the one where my toys are but told me I would have to remove *that* cat, as she so disdainfully put it. *That cat,* I thought. *What a cheek!* Ah, why couldn't she love my lovely, snuggly pussy cat? If only it were real.

Jan and John

Rob and I happened to be in Aberystwyth early one day and, having finished the task at hand, decided to have a late breakfast at Yr Hen Orsaf Wetherspoons.

Sitting at the table next to us were an elderly gentleman and his lady who were engaged in conversation with a younger couple, one of them being their son or daughter, we

assumed. I spied on the back of the gentleman's chair a beautiful, green, knitted scarf. I remarked to Rob that I thought it must be handmade, as the quality was obvious. As they stood up and readied to leave, the gentleman made eye contact with me.

"What a lovely scarf you have!" I said and asked if it was handmade. He said that indeed it was and, what's more, was made on a loom which he had made himself for his good lady.

"Give me your address," he said, "and I'll send details of how to make one." So I did.

After a few days, the postman came with a package for me. Not only did I receive a letter with directions for use, but also included was a loom that the kindly gent had made for me. His name was John and his lady, Jan. He had also enclosed their address and telephone number. Straight away, I called to say, "How very kind indeed," and to invite them for breakfast with us at Wetherspoons. They accepted, and we've been firm friends ever since.

I've made several scarves on my loom. It's used in the same way as I used to do 'French knitting' with four pins on a wooden cotton reel, except that this has thirty pins and shaped like a letterbox instead.

The younger couple that was with John and Jan that day was indeed Jan's daughter, Chris and her husband Dareck. They were visiting from London. They came for another visit a year later, and Jan and John brought them to our house, on my invitation, for afternoon tea. I got on very well with Chris. Being an 'arty' type, like myself, we had plenty to talk about.

John and Jan came to our wedding in 2019. It was held in our garden with the backdrop views of the Cambrian Mountains on a beautiful sunny day in June. After our very informal formalities, John jumped up, wanting to be the one to have the second dance with me. The song was *Brown Sugar* by The Rolling Stones. Goodness me! What energy that man has! He sang, "Yeah, yeah, yeah, woooo,"

and with every 'woooo' came a leg kick and arm swing too, all the while with his big smile. He was 85 then and showed us 'younguns' up good and proper. Jan, being the more reserved one of the two, remained mostly seated but for a slightly less lively dance with Rob.

We see each other on a fairly regular basis. Jan corrects us with our Welsh pronunciations, and they are aplenty, and she tells great 'back-in-the-day' stories, whilst John is an avid writer of poems and stories and documents their many travels. They dropped in on us just last week with a friend who was keenly interested in the gardens and was glad of the encouragement to get a polytunnel. John especially wanted to come to present us with a book in which he'd written a poem about us. He also gave us an owl he'd made from wood. We've named it Obidiya and nailed him to the pergola where we've heard other owls at night. We have many wooden presents handcrafted by John. He's gifted us buttons, a picture frame, several coasters and a couple of ducks. He has a particular fascination for the different patterns and grains he finds within various tree species and just has to make things.

We're so pleased to have met Jan and John, and it just shows how the greatest of friendships can be made on a chance remark.

The Wool-Lined Lanes
of Tynreithin

Cow parsley, Campion and foxgloves grow
Along the wool-lined lanes of Tynreithin
Buzzards, red kites, sparrow hawk and crow
Watch the wool-lined lanes of Tynreithin
The wrens and the swallows, the foxes and hares
Anwen on horseback, Farmer Jones and his heirs
All busy and living out their affairs
On the wool-lined lanes of Tynreithin
A tourist gingerly drives up the hill
On the wool-lined lanes of Tynreithin
An owl hoots loudly when all is still
On the wool-lined lanes of Tynreithin
My love in the house overlooking the bog
The collie and shepherd moving sheep in the fog
I look all around me and I am agog
On the wool-lined lanes of Tynreithin
Postie's red van knows all of the marks
On the wool-lined lanes of Tyreithin
On his day off, Dimelza's dog barks
On the wool-lined lanes of Tynreithin
The bus goes by at ten to four

Drops off the children outside their door
It's shearing time; there are sheep galore
On the wool-lined lanes of Tynreithin.